to Sylvia

THIS IS A BORZOI BOOK PUBLISHED BY ALFRED A. KNOPF

Published in the United States by Alfred A. Knopf, an imprint of Random House Children's Books, a division of Random House, Inc., New York. Originally published in Great Britain in 2005 by Andersen Press Ltd., London.

KNOPF, BORZOI BOOKS, and the colophon are registered trademarks of Random House, Inc.

www.randomhouse.com/kids

Educators and librarians, for a variety of teaching tools, visit us at
www.randomhouse.com/teachers

Library of Congress Cataloging-in-Publication Data
Lucas, David.
Nutmeg / by David Lucas. — 1st American ed.
p. cm.
SUMMARY: Bored with her meals of cardboard, string, and sawdust, Nutmeg acquires from a genie a magic spoon to make some different dishes but winds up with more than she bargained for.
ISBN 0-375-83519-9 (trade) — ISBN 0-375-93519-3 (lib. bdg.)
[1. Genies—Fiction. 2. Magic—Fiction. 3. Spoons—Fiction.] I. Title.
PZ7.L96895Nut 2006
[E]—dc22   2005015785

PRINTED IN ITALY

August 2006

10 9 8 7 6 5 4 3 2 1

First American Edition

nutmeg

by David Lucas

Alfred A. Knopf

New York

There was *always* cardboard for breakfast.

There was *always* string for lunch.

There was *always* sawdust for supper.

The living room was full of junk.
Nutmeg looked out of the window.
Cousin Nesbit fiddled with bits of things.
Uncle Nicodemus sat in his chair and dozed.

Nutmeg stood up.

"I am going for a *walk*," she said.

"Why?" said Cousin Nesbit.

"Whatever for?" said Uncle Nicodemus.

"I don't *know*!" said Nutmeg.

But she went for a walk nevertheless.

Nutmeg walked to the creek.
She sat and watched the tide come in.

What was that?
There was a bottle at the water's edge.

There seemed to be a tiny light inside.
Nutmeg opened the bottle.

Out burst a genie.

"I have been trapped for a thousand years,"
said the Genie. "You have set me free.
In return I shall grant you three wishes."
"Three wishes?" said Nutmeg.
"Yes," said the Genie. "Now come on . . .
what do you want?"
"But I don't *know* what I want," she said.
"Of course you do. Just think!"
Nutmeg thought.
"Come on . . . *come on!*" said the Genie.
"I would very much like something *different* for
supper," said Nutmeg, at last.
"And?"
". . . and something *different* for breakfast."
"And?"
". . . and something *different* for lunch."

"There!" said the Genie, and handed her
a spoon, a magic spoon.
Then, in a flash
and a bang,
he was gone.

Nutmeg hurried home.

The Spoon conjured up all kinds of ingredients.

The Spoon cooked supper all by itself.

And that night they all went to sleep with a smile.

In the night
Nutmeg heard a noise:

Bing

BANG

Bong!

Clatter

Clatter

CRASH!

Nutmeg crept
downstairs.

The Spoon wasn't cooking.
The Spoon was stirring up the kitchen.

Bang Bang Clatter *CRASH!*

"Stop it!" said Nutmeg. "STOP IT!"

Uncle Nicodemus hurried onto the landing.
Cousin Nesbit slid down the banister.

The Spoon stirred up the living room.

"Behave yourself, Master Spoon!"
said Uncle Nicodemus.
Cousin Nesbit shook his fist.

The Spoon stirred up the *whole* house.
"Hold tight!" said Uncle Nicodemus.

The Spoon stirred up the land and sea.
The Spoon mixed up the stars.

Nutmeg dared not look.
"Be brave now, shipmates!"
said Uncle Nicodemus. "Be brave!"

Splash!

The wind was soft, the sun was rising,
and the Spoon was nowhere to be seen.

Nutmeg took the wheel.
Cousin Nesbit hoisted the flag.
"Land ho!" cried Uncle Nicodemus.

"Something different for breakfast too!"
said Nutmeg.

And after breakfast they set sail again, and it wasn't long before Nutmeg began to wonder what they'd have for *lunch*.